ANDERSEN'S FAIRY TALES

Translated and adapted by
KATHERINE FOLLIOT

Illustrated by
PAUL DURAND

DERRYDALE BOOKS

NEW YORK

Contents

First published in 1972
By Editions des Deux Coqs d'Or, Paris
under the title: *Contes d'Andersen*

©1972 by Editions des Deux Coqs d'Or, Paris

This 1988 edition published
by Derrydale Books, distributed by Crown Publishers, Inc.,
225 Park Avenue South, New York, New York 10003,
by arrangement with Octopus Books Limited.

Printed by Mladinska knjiga, Yugoslavia

ISBN 0–517–67135–2

h g f e d c b a

THE SHEPHERDESS AND THE CHIMNEY SWEEP

Have you ever seen one of those antique wooden cupboards, sculpted all over and quite black with age? Well, just such a cupboard, no doubt a legacy from somebody's great-great-grandmother, once stood in a room. It was decorated with carved tulips and roses and with little harts' heads, complete with antlers. In the centre of this cabinet the artist had sculpted a strange, human-like figure; a creature with a permanent grin on its face, goat's legs, short horns and a long beard. The children of the house called him 'Major-General Commander-in-Chief Billygoat-leg', a long and difficult title maybe, but almost certainly one that no-one else has ever had. Well, there he was, his eyes permanently fixed on the console-table under the big mirror, where stood a little china shepherdess. With her golden slippers, her pretty dress adorned with a fresh rosebud, her gilded hat and her tiny crook, she looked quite charming. Next to her stood a little chimney-sweep, also made of china, who, despite the fact that he was black as coal, was really as nice and clean as you and me, for he was only the replica of a chimney-sweep. The china manufacturer might just as well have made him a prince; it would have made very little difference.

The chimney-sweep held his ladder very gracefully and his face was as pink and white as that of a girl – a slight mistake which could perhaps have been avoided by adding a dab of black paint. He could almost touch the shepherdess. Somebody had once placed them right next to each other and, because they were so close, they had become engaged. They were really quite well suited, for both of them were made of china and both were equally fragile and delicate.

Not very far from them stood another porcelain figure which was three times as large; an old Chinaman who could nod his head. Although he had never been able to prove it, the Chinaman claimed to be the little shepherdess's grandfather and, as such, to have complete power over her. That is why, when Major-General Commander-in-Chief Billygoatleg asked for the hand of the little shepherdess in marriage, the old man gave his approval with an amiable nod.

'What a catch! What a catch!' he kept repeating. 'I do believe your suitor is made of real mahogany. He will make you "Lady Major-General Commander-in-Chief Billygoatleg". His cabinet is full of silverware and goodness knows what he hoards in his secret drawer.'

'I will never go into that dark cupboard,' said the little shepherdess; 'I have heard it said that there are eleven china ladies in there.'

'Well, you will be the twelfth,' replied the Chinaman. 'To-night, as soon as the old thing starts to creak, we will celebrate your wedding, as sure as I am a Chinaman.' And upon these words he nodded and fell fast asleep. The little shepherdess looked at her chimney-sweep and started to cry.

'Please help me to run away into the big wide world,' she pleaded. 'We can no longer stay here.'

10

'Your word is my command,' the sweep replied. 'Let us escape at once. With a trade such as mine I am sure that I can take good care of you.'

'Let's hope it isn't too difficult to climb down from the table,' she said. 'I shan't feel safe until we are far from here.'

He comforted her and showed her where to put her little feet on the gilded mouldings of the table leg. With the additional help of his ladder they soon reached the floor safely. However, as they turned round to glance at the old cabinet, they saw that everything there was in an uproar: all the harts were craning their necks and straining their antlers to watch their escape and Major-General Commander-in-Chief Billygoatleg was quivering with rage and screaming at the old Chinaman: 'They are running away! They are running away!'

The little figures were so frightened by this that they ran and hid in the drawer of the window-seat.

In there they found three or four incomplete sets of playing-cards and a little toy theatre. A play was in progress at that very moment. Regardless of whether they belonged to the diamond, spade, heart or club family, all the queens were seated in the front row, fanning themselves with their tulips. Behind them stood the knaves, with one head up and one head down, as they are on playing-cards. The play was about two young lovers who could not get married and it made the shepherdess cry a lot, for it reminded her too vividly of her own predicament.

'This is too sad,' she said; 'I must get out of this drawer.' But as soon as they had stepped out again on to the floor and looked up at the console-table they saw that the old Chinaman had woken up and was pointing and waving at them wildly.

'The old man is coming after us!' cried the little shepherdess, and in her fright she fell down, on her porcelain knees.

'I have an idea,' said the chimney-sweep. 'Let's hide inside the big Jug over there in the corner. We can rest there, among the flowers and if he comes after us we can throw some water at him.'

'No, that wouldn't work,' she answered. 'I know that the old Chinaman and the Jug were engaged once and in such cases a bond of friendship always remains, even after many years. No, our only hope is to escape into the big wide world.'

'Do you really feel up to that?' asked the chimney-sweep. 'Do you realize that the big wide world is very big indeed and that we may never be able to come back here again?'

'I realize it perfectly well!' she retorted. The chimney-sweep looked at her intently for a moment, then he said:

'In my opinion, the best way out would be through the chimney. Do you feel brave enough to climb into the stove and up the stove-pipe after me? That is the only way we can reach the chimney flue and once we are there I shall know exactly what to do. We shall have to climb up to the very top of the chimney until we reach the hole which opens on to the outside world.'

He led her by the hand to the stove door.

'Goodness! How dark it is in here!' she shuddered.

All the same she followed him in and walked along the pipe in the darkness.

'We are now in the chimney,' he said. 'Look at the lovely star up there.'

The light of the star helped them to find their way, as they climbed higher and higher. It was a long and difficult journey, but he never left her side and showed her the best footholds for her little china feet.

At long last they reached the chimney-stack and they sat down on the ledge for a rest, for they were completely exhausted after their long ascent.

Hundreds of stars twinkled in the sky above them and far down below they could see the sloping roofs of the entire city. They looked all around them at the big wide world. The little shepherdess had never imagined that it could be so vast. In her dismay she put her head on the chimney-sweep's shoulder and began to weep so hard that her tears stained the little jerkin.

'This is too much!' she wailed. 'It is more than I can bear. The big wide world is really much too big. I wish I were back on the console-table by the big mirror. I shall never be happy until I am back there again. I followed you into the big wide world; now, if you really love me, you must take me back home.'

The chimney-sweep tried to reason with her. He reminded her of the old Chinaman and of Major-General Commander-in-Chief Billygoatleg, but she sobbed so hard and kissed him so tenderly that he gave in to her, even though he knew it was madness to do so.

With much difficulty they made the return journey down the chimney, through the pipe and into the dark stove. It wasn't much fun at all. When they reached the stove door they stopped and listened, but all was quiet in the room so they peeped out to have a look round.

Alas! The old Chinaman lay broken on the floor. When he had tried to run after them he had fallen off the table and broken into three pieces. His back was severed from the rest of his body and his

head had rolled off into a corner. Major-General Commander-in-Chief Billygoatleg was still in the same position as before and appeared to be lost in thought.

'This is terrible!' the little shepherdess cried. 'Old Grandfather is in pieces and it is all our fault. Oh! I shall never get over it!' and she wrung her little hands.

'He can be stuck together again,' said the chimney-sweep. 'I am sure he can be stuck together again. Don't fret. Once his back has been glued to his front and his head secured back on with a strong rivet he will be as good as new, and he'll be able to say all sorts of disagreeable things to us once again.'

'Do you really think so?' she said. They climbed back on to the console-table where they had always lived.

'Well, here we are again,' said the sweep. 'There was really not much point in going to so much trouble.'

'Oh! If only old Grandfather could be mended!' the shepherdess went on. 'Would it cost an awful lot of money?' So the old Grandfather was mended and with the help of a strong rivet he became as good as new; except that he could no longer nod his head.

'You have become very haughty since your accident,' Major-General Commander-in-Chief Billygoatleg observed. 'I don't know that you have any reason to look so stiff. But be that as it may, will you consent to my proposal or won't you?'

The chimney-sweep and the shepherdess looked appealingly at the old Chinaman, for they were terrified that he would nod his consent.

But, thanks to the rivet, he could no longer nod and as he would have been too ashamed to admit it, the little china sweethearts were able to stay together until their dying day – or rather until the day when they, too, were broken.

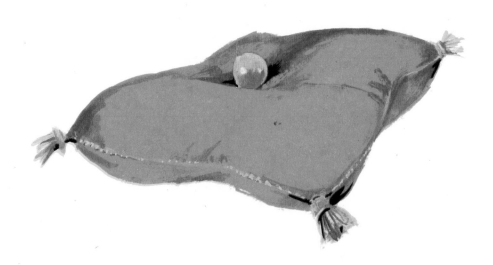

THE PRINCESS AND THE PEA

Once upon a time there lived a prince who wanted to get married, but insisted that he would only marry a real princess. He toured the whole world in search of one and indeed found that princesses were very plentiful, but he could never be sure that they were real princesses; he always felt that there was something wrong somewhere. So he returned home very sad and disappointed.

One dreadful stormy night as thunder and lightning shook the heavens and rain poured down in bucketfuls, someone knocked on the door of the castle and the old king himself hurried to see who it might be.

A princess stood there in the rain. She was in a terrible state; her hair and clothes were soaking wet and water trickled out of her shoes, but she said she was a real princess.

'Well, we shall soon see about that!' thought the queen, and, without saying a word, she went into the guest bedroom, removed all the bedclothes from the bed and put a pea on the bedstead. Then she put twenty mattresses over the pea and twenty eiderdowns on top of the mattresses.

This was the bed the princess was given for the night. The next morning she was asked how she had slept.

'Very badly, I am afraid,' she said. 'I could hardly close my eyes at all. Goodness knows what was in my bed, but it was so hard that I am bruised all over. It was real torture.'

This proved beyond any doubt that she was indeed a real princess. She had felt a single pea through twenty mattresses and twenty eiderdowns; who could have so delicate a skin, apart from a genuine princess?

Convinced that he had at last found his real princess, the prince made her his wife and the pea was placed in a museum, where it may well be to this day if it has not been pinched by a curio lover.

This is a true story, as true as the princess herself.

THE
UGLY
DUCKLING

It was high summer and the countryside was at its loveliest. The corn was golden, the oats were green and big fragrant haystacks stood in the meadows. A stork strutted about on its long reddish legs, chatting all the while in Egyptian, the language it had learned from its mother. Fields and meadows were enclosed by thick forests and deep lakes lay in the forests.

Yes, the countryside was beautiful indeed. The sun shone brightly on an old mansion and its surrounding moat. Dock leaves grew from the walls of the house down to the water's edge; they were so tall that little children could hide under them and they provided as wild and impenetrable a cover as the thickest wood. This was the hide-out a mother duck had chosen to build her nest and sit on her eggs. She was eager to see her babies hatch, for she had been there a long time and was getting rather bored. She had had few visitors, as the other ducks preferred to paddle in the moat rather than come and gossip with her under the dock leaves.

At last the eggs started to crack, one after the other. 'Cheep, Cheep,' the little ducklings said as they greeted life and peeped out of their shells.

Then they started to quack as loud as they could and peered all around them under the green dock leaves. Their mother let them peer to their hearts' content, for green is good for the eyes.

'How big the world is!' marvelled the newly-born as they left the confines of their eggs.

'You think this is the whole world?' chirped their mother. 'That is not so. The world goes much further, to the other side of the garden, all the way to the parson's field, although I must admit I have never been there myself.

'Are you all out now?' she enquired, standing up. 'No, the biggest egg is still here. Oh dear! How long this is taking! I am so tired of waiting.' And she sat down again, looking rather peeved.

'Well, my dear, how are you?' quacked an old duck who came to visit her.

'There is only one left and it just won't crack,' she replied, 'but look at the others. Aren't they the sweetest ducklings you ever saw? They all look remarkably like their father, yet the rascal has not come to see us once.'

'Show me this egg which will not crack,' said the old duck. 'Ah! Believe me, this is a turkey's egg. I too was fooled once, just like you, and I had great trouble with the chick, for those creatures are terrified of water. I simply could not make it go in. I even carried it in and showed it how to paddle, but it was no use. Let me have another look. Yes, this is definitely a turkey's egg. You should just leave it and teach your other children how to swim.'

'I have already wasted so much time that I may as well wait another day or two,' the mother duck retorted.

'Well, suit yourself,' quacked the old duck and she waddled off.

The big egg cracked at last and the chick chirped 'Cheep-Cheep' as it came out. But it was big and ugly and the mother pondered as she looked at it: 'What a huge creature this is. It doesn't look like any of us. Could it really be a turkey chick? We shall soon see. It will go into the water, if I have to drag it there.'

The next day, as the weather was good and the sun was shining on the green dock leaves, the mother took all her ducklings to the water's edge. She jumped in with a splash and then, at her command 'Quack, Quack', they all jumped in, one after the other. The water closed over them, but they soon came up again and then started to swim vigorously. Their little legs paddled away and they all thoroughly enjoyed the water, even the big, ugly grey duckling.

'This is no turkey chick,' thought the mother duck. 'How cleverly it uses its legs and how upright it holds it head. It must be one of my own chicks after all. Anyway, it isn't all that ugly really. Quack, quack!' she went on. 'Now, come with me. I will take you into the world and introduce you to the farmyard. But make sure you stay close to me, so that nobody treads on you, and beware of the cat.'

They all trooped into the farmyard.

What a din there was in there! Two broods were quarrelling over an eel's head and in the end it was the cat who got it.

'That's how things go in this world,' sighed the duck and she licked her bill, for she too would have dearly liked a piece of eel's head.

'Now walk along. Keep together and go and pay your respects to the old duck over there. She is the most distinguished duck here. She is of Spanish origin, which is why she is so fat. Take note of the red ribbon round her leg; that is the highest distinction a duck can have. It shows it is valuable and worthy of respect. Behave yourselves now. Don't turn your feet inwards; a well-bred duckling always points its feet outwards, like so. Now, bow your heads and say "Quack".'

The ducklings did as they were told, but the ducks in the yard stared at them and exclaimed, 'Oh dear! More ducklings. As if there weren't enough of us already. Fie, Fie, what kind of duckling is this? We can't have that here.' Whereupon a big duck flew at the ugly duckling and bit it in the neck.

'Leave him alone!' said the mother duck. 'He does no harm.'

'Maybe so,' said the attacker, 'but he is so big and so ridiculous that he deserves a good thrashing.'

'Those are fine ducklings you have there, Mother duck,' said the old duck with the red ribbon. 'They are all handsome, apart from that one. There is something wrong with him I fear and I wish that you could re-make him.'

'That is not possible, Your Ladyship. I admit he is not handsome, but he has a very good temper and he swims as well as the others, if not better. I think his looks will improve as grows up. He just stayed too long in his egg, that's all,' and she patted and stroked the duckling as she spoke. 'Besides,' she added, 'he is a male, so I don't think beauty is so important. I am sure he will be strong and make his way in the world.'

'Well, the other ones are pretty, anyway. So do make yourselves at home and if you find an eel's head bring it to me.'

They made themselves at home, but the poor duckling who had been last to hatch was pecked and mocked and jeered by everybody, even the hens.

'He is much too big!' they kept saying; and the turkey-cock, who had been born with spurs and therefore thought himself very important, fluffed himself up like a ship in full sail and advanced upon him, red with anger. The poor duckling did not know whether he should move or stay still. He was very sad to be so ugly and to be the laughing stock of the whole farmyard.

After this first unhappy day, things went from bad to worse. The poor duckling was rejected by everyone. Even his brothers and sisters were mean to him and said they wished the cat would rid them of him and his own mother sometimes said she wished he could be far away. The ducks bit him, the hens pecked him and the maid who brought them food always kicked him aside.

So he ran away. As he hopped over the hedge the little birds in it took to their wings in fright. 'That's because I am so ugly,' he thought sadly, but he shut his eyes and went on. He finally stopped by the great marsh where the wild ducks lived and, completely exhausted, lay down for the night.

The next morning, when the wild ducks awoke and saw him there, they enquired who he might be. The duckling turned round in all directions and bowed as politely as he could.

'You are extremely ugly,' the wild ducks said, 'but that does not matter to us, as long as you don't marry anyone in our family.'

Poor wretch! As if he could be thinking of marriage. All he asked was to be allowed to lie among the reeds and to drink a little water from the marsh.

He lay there for two whole days. Then two young wild ganders arrived. They had not long been out of their eggs and, consequently, were rather cocksure.

'Look here, old chap,' they said to the duckling, 'your ugliness is not devoid of charm. Will you join us and become a bird of passage? Very close to here, in the next marsh, there are some charming wild geese who have lovely voices and are nearly all single. Ugly as you are, you might have a chance there.'

Suddenly a shot rang out: 'Bang!' The two ganders fell down
dead among the reeds and the water turned blood-red.

'Bang-Bang!' Flocks of wild geese flew up from the bulrushes and
more shots were fired. It was a big shoot; the sportsmen lay in wait
all round the marsh; some even lay on low-lying branches right over
the edge. Clouds of blue smoke came out from among the trees and
slowly disappeared over the water; then dogs waded into the swamp
and splashed about among the reeds and the bulrushes. The poor

duckling was terrified. He was about to hide his head under his wing when he saw a huge dog right in front of him. Its tongue was hanging out and its eyes glared wildly at him. It pointed its muzzle towards the duckling, bared its teeth and then, 'Splash, Splash', went away again.

'Thank goodness!' sighed the little duck. 'I am so ugly that even dogs won't touch me.' He lay as still as he could, while the bullets whistled through the bushes and the shots rang out incessantly.

Towards evening the noise died down, but even then the poor creature did not dare move. He waited for several hours before looking around and then he ran away from the marsh as fast as he could.

Despite strong winds he hurried across fields and meadows and by evening he reached an old derelict cottage which only remained standing because it did not know which way to fall. The gale blew so hard that the poor duckling had to stop and squat down low to resist it. But it grew worse and worse.

He noticed that one of the cottage doors had partly come off its hinges and he crept in through the small opening.

In the cottage dwelt an old woman, a tom-cat and a hen. The cat, which the old woman called 'Sonny', knew how to arch its back and purr; it could even make sparks when its back was rubbed the wrong way. The hen had very short legs and, for that reason, had been nicknamed 'Shortie'. She laid excellent eggs and the old woman loved her like a daughter.

The following day the presence of the intruder was discovered. The tom-cat hissed and the hen started to cluck.

'What is the matter?' asked the old woman and she peered around to see, but her eyesight was not very good so that she mistook the creature for a stray duck. 'What a good catch!' she chuckled, 'now I shall have some duck's eggs – that is if the creature is not a drake. Well, let's give it a try.' After three weeks however there were still no eggs.

The tom-cat and the hen were the masters in this household and they had acquired the habit of saying 'We and the world,' for they firmly believed that they constituted one half (the better in fact) of the world. The duckling ventured to think otherwise, but this angered the hen.

'Can you lay eggs?' she asked.

'No,' he replied.

'Well then, kindly keep quiet.'

Then it was the turn of the tom-cat. 'Can you arch your back? Can you purr or make sparks?' he said.

'No.'

'Then you have no right to express an opinion when more sensible people are talking.'

The duckling sat alone in his corner, feeling rather miserable, when suddenly the thought of sunshine and fresh air came into his head and he felt a strong desire to go swimming. He could not help telling the hen about it.

'What are you talking about?' said the hen. 'You do nothing all day long, that is why you have these wild fancies. Lay some eggs or purr and you'll find they will pass.'

'But it is such fun to float on the water and then to dive right under, to the very bottom.'

'Great fun I'm sure,' clucked the hen. 'I think you must be slightly mad. Ask the cat, who is the most sensible creature I know, whether he enjoys floating on the water or diving under it. Ask the old mistress if you like – no one in the world could be more experienced than she. Do you think that she would enjoy floating or diving?'

'You don't understand,' said the duckling.

'We don't understand? Who on earth could understand you? Do you by any chance think that you are cleverer than the cat or the mistress, not to mention myself? Don't delude yourself child. You

should be thankful for the kindness that was bestowed on you, for the warm room and the interesting company, instead of arguing and making a nuisance of yourself. It is no pleasure to live with you. Believe me, I wish you well; I may say unpleasant things, but that is how one recognizes real friends. Try to lay some eggs, or learn how to purr.'

'I think I will return to the outside world,' said the duckling.

'Well, as you wish,' said the chicken.

So the duckling returned to the outside world. He floated on the water and dived as much as he liked, but he was scorned by every animal for his ugliness.

Autumn came; the leaves in the forest turned yellow and brown and fluttered in the wind. The air was very cold and dark clouds, full of hail and snow, filled the sky. The raven croaked, half frozen on his perch, and the sound made everyone shiver. In truth the poor duckling was not very happy.

One evening, as the sun was setting, a flock of magnificent birds came out of the thicket. The duckling had never yet seen anything so beautiful. The birds were dazzling white, they had long graceful necks and they uttered a strange cry as they flapped their strong wings and soared high up in the sky. These were swans, on their way to warmer lands. The ugly duckling suddenly felt strangely moved.

He turned a cartwheel in the water, craned his little neck in the air towards the travellers and uttered such a strange and piercing shriek that he was quite frightened by it himself. He would never forget these beautiful and happy-looking birds. When they had disappeared from sight he dived as deep as he could and when he surfaced again he was beside himself with excitement. He did not know the name of these birds, nor where they were going, yet he loved them as he had never loved anyone before.

He was not jealous of their beauty; such a thought never entered his head. The poor ungainly creature would have been pleased enough to be tolerated by ducks.

Winter came and the cold became so bitter that the duckling had to swim all the time to avoid being frozen in the ice. Every night the hole in which he swam grew smaller and smaller.

The poor duckling paddled non-stop, but he became so tired that
he could no longer move and, eventually, he was trapped.

Fortunately, the next morning a peasant passed by and saw what
had happened. He walked on to the ice, freed the duckling and took
him home to his wife. Once indoors the little duck came back to life.

The children tried to play with him, but he was afraid of them
so he jumped into the milk churn for safety. Milk spurted all over
the floor and the angry housewife clapped her hands. This frightened the duckling even more, so he flew into the butter-churn and
then into the flour bin. When he came out he really looked a sight!
The woman screamed and tried to hit him with the firetongs. The
children laughed and shouted and fell on top of each other in their

efforts to catch him. Fortunately the door was open and he was able to escape. He flew out into the bushes and huddled in the snow, utterly exhausted.

It would be too sad to relate how much misery and suffering he had to bear during that severe winter.

He lay among the bulrushes in the marsh until at last the sun became warmer and brighter, the larks began to sing and a lovely spring began.

When he shook his wings again the duckling found that they were much more powerful than they had been before. He flapped them vigorously and started to fly, easily and effortlessly. After flying for some time he stopped in a large garden where apple trees were in full blossom and where the green branches of sweet-smelling lilacs hung low over the banks of a narrow lake. Everything there was beautiful and fresh.

Three magnificent white swans emerged from the bushes.

They flapped their wings and glided elegantly on the water. The duckling recognized the beautiful birds and he was filled with a sense of hopeless longing.

'I will approach these regal birds,' he thought. 'They will no doubt kill me since I am such an ugly creature, but I don't mind. I would rather be killed by them than be bitten by ducks, pecked by chickens, kicked by farm maids and suffer the miseries of winter.'

He flew to the water's edge and swam towards the swans. They saw him and rushed forward, ruffling their feathers.

'Kill me,' said the poor little bird; and he bowed his head, expecting death.

But what did he suddenly see in the clear water? He saw his own reflection and it was no longer that of a drab, ugly bird; it was that of a swan!

What does it matter if one was born among ducks, when the egg from which one hatched was a swan's egg. His trials and tribulations had not been in vain, for they made the joy of his wonderful discovery all the greater. For the first time in his life he felt the taste of happiness, as the older swans swam round him and stroked him gently with their beaks.

Some little children came into the garden and started throwing bread and corn at the birds in the water. The youngest one suddenly cried out, 'Look, there's a new swan!' And the others rejoiced and said, 'Yes, another swan has come.' They clapped their hands and skipped about excitedly and then ran to their parents to get more food for the birds. Everyone agreed that the new swan was the most beautiful and the most graceful of all.

At this point all the old swans bowed to him.

This made him feel embarrassed and he shyly hid his head under his wing, not knowing what to do. He was enormously happy, but not in the least proud of his new-found beauty.

Not so long ago, he reflected, he had found nothing but mockery and sorrow everywhere; now, everyone said that he was the most beautiful of all beautiful birds. The lilacs themselves bent their fragrant branches towards him and the friendly sun gave out light and warmth. Brimming over with joy, the little swan ruffled his feathers, stretched his slender neck and said, 'I never even dreamt that such happiness could exist when I was nothing but an ugly duckling.'

THE
LITTLE
TIN
SOLDIER

Once upon a time there were twenty-five tin soldiers who were all brothers, for they had all been cast from the same old tin spoon. They looked very brave in their red and blue uniforms, with their rifles at the ready and their fixed expression. The first thing they ever heard in this world was the joyous cry 'Hurrah! Some tin soldiers!' uttered by a delighted little boy when he lifted the lid off their box. They were his birthday present and he had much fun with them, arranging them in various positions on the table. All the soldiers were identical apart from one, who had only one leg; he had been the last of the batch and there had not been quite enough tin left to finish him. Nevertheless he stood as upright on his leg as the others on two and it was he who had the most interesting adventures.

There were many other toys on the table besides the soldiers. The most remarkable of them was a miniature cardboard castle; through its tiny windows one could see right inside the rooms and, close to it, miniature trees surrounded a lake, made out of a piece of mirror, with wax swans on it. It was all very sweet, but the sweetest thing of all was the little lady who stood before the open door. She too

was cut out of cardboard. Her tutu was made of gauze and, by way of a scarf, she wore a little piece of narrow blue ribbon pinned with a sequin as big as her face. The little lady held her arms up in the air, for she was a dancer and one of her legs was raised so high that the little tin soldier could not see it, so he thought that she too had only one leg.

'Just the right woman for me,' he thought. 'Unfortunately, she is too highly born. She lives in a castle, whereas I live in a box, with twenty-four comrades. She would not fit in there. Still, I can try to make her acquaintance.'

Thereupon, he lay down behind a snuff-box and closely watched the graceful lady who stood permanently on her one leg, without ever losing her balance.

In the evening all the other tin soldiers were put back in their box and the people of the house went to bed. This was the time when the toys could play. They played blind man's buff, then soldiers and, finally, they had a dance. The tin soldiers fidgeted in their box for they would have loved to join in the fun, but the lid was tightly shut. The nutcracker turned somersaults, the pencil scribbled on its slate and, awakened by all the noise, the canary started to sing. The only ones who did not move were the little tin soldier and the little dancer. She stood still on one foot with arms outstretched and he, on his one leg, looked at her fixedly.

The clock struck twelve and suddenly the snuff-box burst open; instead of snuff it contained a wizard Jack-in-the-Box.

'Tin soldier,' said the wizard, 'kindly look somewhere else'. But the tin soldier pretended not to hear.

'Just wait till tomorrow,' muttered the wizard. On the morrow, when the children got up, they put the tin soldier on the window-sill and either a magic spell or a gust of wind suddenly blew him out, so that he fell head first on to the pavement three floors below. It was a terrifying fall.

He landed upside down, on his busby, with his one leg in the air and his bayonet stuck between two paving-stones.

The little boy and his maid came running down to get him back but they could not see anything and very nearly trod on him. They would no doubt have discovered him had he shouted out, but he felt it would be improper to shout while in uniform, so he remained silent.

It started to rain. The drops fell thick and fast and quickly turned into a downpour. When the storm abated two street urchins came by:

'Look!' said one of them, 'a tin soldier. Let's make him a boat.'

They made a boat out of an old newspaper, placed the little soldier in it and set it afloat in the gutter. They clapped excitedly and ran alongside as it sailed down on the swift current. The water was high because of the storm, so that the paper boat bobbed up and down and whirled round and round at full speed.

Despite the swell the tin soldier stayed calm; he held his rifle up and gazed straight ahead.

Suddenly the boat shot into a dark tunnel, as dark as the tin soldier's box.

'Where am I going now?' he wondered. 'I have the wizard to thank for all this unpleasantness. Yet, if the little lady were here with me,' he reflected, 'I wouldn't care if it were twice as dark.'

Presently a fat water rat who lived in the tunnel came up to him and said, 'Passport please.'

The tin soldier did not budge and said nothing. The boat sailed on and the rat scurried after it, gnashing his teeth with rage and shouting to all passing flotsam: 'Stop him, stop him! He hasn't shown his pass. He hasn't paid the toll!'

The current grew stronger and stronger. The soldier could see light at the end of the tunnel, but at the same time he heard a roaring sound which would have frightened the bravest of the brave.

Where the tunnel ended the water poured into a big canal in a gushing waterfall which was as ominous for him as a mighty cataract would be for us. The boat had to go on. As it fell over the waterfall the brave little soldier kept his rigid posture and did not even blink. The boat spun round and round, filled with water up to the soldier's neck and started to sink.

As the paper got more waterlogged it sank altogether and the water closed over the soldier's head. He thought of his pretty little dancer whom he would never see again and heard a voice saying:

'Fear not, fear not, noble soldier,
Even though grim death be near.'

At this point the paper tore, the soldier fell through and a large fish instantly swallowed him.

It was darker inside the fish than it had been in the tunnel and a great deal tighter, but the tin soldier's courage did not desert him and he stayed as upright as ever.

The fish twisted and turned and wriggled frantically. Then it stopped moving. A flash seemed to run straight through it, then light appeared and someone exclaimed: 'A tin soldier!' The fish had been caught, taken to market, sold and brought into a kitchen, where the cook had slit it open with a sharp knife. With two fingers

she seized the tin soldier by his middle and carried him to the nursery, where everyone wanted to have a look at the hero who had travelled inside the belly of a fish; but this did not go to the soldier's head. He was placed on a table and immediately realized that by some extraordinary trick of fate he had returned to the very room which had formerly been his home.

He recognized the children and the toys on the table. The lovely castle was there and the little dancer, with her leg high up in the air, was just the same as ever. The tin soldier was so moved that

he could have cried tin tears, but it would have been unseemly for a soldier to cry, so he didn't. They just looked at each other, without saying a word.

Then all of a sudden, for no apparent reason, one of the boys took hold of the soldier and threw him into the fire. No doubt this was the wizard's work.

The tin soldier stood upright in the blazing heat. Whether from emotion or as a result of his adventures, his colour had all gone, but he went on gazing at the little lady and she at him; and although he could feel he was starting to melt, he remained as upright as he could. Suddenly a door was opened and the little dancer was caught in a draught. She flew like a sylph into the fire, right next to the soldier and in a second had entirely burnt away. All that was left of her was her blackened sequin.

The soldier melted into a little lump of tin. The next morning, when the maid came to empty the ashes from the grate, she found a little lump in the shape of a heart.

THUMBELINA

There once was a woman whose one desire was to have a child but she could not have one. So she went to an old witch and said, 'I would dearly like a little child. What can I do to have one?'

'It is not very difficult,' answered the witch. 'Take this seed which is different from the sort one sows in the fields or gives to chickens. Plant it in a flower-pot and you will soon see what happens.'

The woman thanked the witch, gave her twelve pence and then went home to plant the seed.

A beautiful, tall flower quickly grew from the seed; it looked rather like a tulip. 'What a pretty bud,' exclaimed the woman. She kissed the little bundle of red and yellow petals and instantly the bud burst open. In the green middle of the tulip sat a delicate and tiny maiden, no bigger than her thumb, and because of her size she was given the name of Thumbelina.

A polished walnut shell became her cot and there she slept at night, on a mattress made of violet leaves, with a rose petal for a blanket. During the day she played on the table, in a bowl of flowers the woman had placed there. A big tulip petal which floated on the surface made a perfect boat for Thumbelina; she would sit on it and row from side to side with oars made out of two white horsehairs. A most charming sight! She could also sing and her melodious, gentle voice was without compare.

One night, while she was sleeping, an enormous, slimy toad came into the room through a broken window pane and jumped on to the table where Thumbelina lay snugly under her rose petal.

'What a pretty wife this would make my son,' thought the toad. He seized the walnut shell, leapt back through the hole in the window and carried the little maiden into the garden.

The toad lived with his son on the marshy bank of the stream which ran through the garden; and the son was just as hideous and slimy as the father. When he saw the maiden in her shell he croaked excitedly.

'Don't croak so loudly,' warned the old toad. 'She could wake up and run away as lightly as swansdown. We must place her on a water-lily leaf in the middle of the stream. To her this will seem as big as an island and she won't be able to escape while we get your married quarters ready in the mud patch.'

The toad swam to the green water-lily which was farthest from the shore and there he left Thumbelina, still asleep in her walnut shell.

When the poor little maiden woke up the next morning and saw where she was she cried bitterly, for there was water on all sides and she had no means of reaching the shore.

After decorating the couple's future home with reeds and little yellow flowers, the old toad swam back to the water-lily to collect the walnut bed. He bowed very formally to Thumbelina and explained that she and his son were to be married and that a beautiful home would soon be ready for them.

'Croak-Croak!' added the son.

They took the bed and swam away, leaving Thumbelina alone and disconsolate on the green leaf. The thought of marrying the horrible toad filled her with disgust and she wept piteously.

The fishes in the stream had heard what the toad had said and they felt curious about the maiden. They peeped out to have a look at her and found her delightful. She was much too pretty to marry the ugly toad! Something must be done to prevent it! They gathered round the stalk which anchored the water-lily to the ground and gnawed right through it, so that the green leaf floated away downstream, far from the loathsome toads.

The leaf travelled on and on and took Thumbelina to far-away places. The maiden was thrilled to have escaped from the toads and delighted by the beauty of the landscape and the sparkling waters.

As she passed by, the birds on the bank would sing, 'What a pretty maid,' and somewhere on the way a lovely butterfly flew up and fluttered its white wings admiringly at her. When it came closer still and alighted near her the maiden untied her belt and attached one end of it to the butterfly, the other to the leaf, so as to go even faster.

A stag-beetle who was passing by saw the maiden and took a fancy to her. Without further ado he snatched her up and carried her into a tree, while the green leaf continued its journey downstream, together with the butterfly.

Poor little Thumbelina was petrified with fear at being carried up into a tree, but she was even more sorry for the white butterfly who would surely die of hunger if he could not get loose from the leaf to which she had attached him. The stag-beetle, however, cared little for the butterfly. He seated the maiden on a large leaf, brought her some nectar for refreshment and proceeded to pay her compliments, even though she looked in no way like a stag-beetle.

Soon the other stag-beetles in the tree came to pay her a visit. When they saw her the females shrugged their feelers and said, 'Only two legs!'

One of them added, 'And no feelers! And her waist is as narrow as that of a human. What an ugly creature!'

In truth Thumbelina was very beautiful and the stag-beetle who had abducted her found her so, but when he heard all the others say that she was ugly, he came to believe them and lost interest in her. He took her away from the tree and set her down on a daisy below.

Despite her new-found freedom, it made the little maiden cry to think she was so ugly. She could not tell it wasn't true.

She spent the whole summer alone in the big forest. She made herself a bed of twigs under a big leaf, to shelter from the rain, and sustained herself with nectar and with dew.

Summer and autumn passed, and then came winter; a long, hard winter. The birds who had entertained her with their songs flew away, the trees lost their foliage, the flowers died and the big leaf which had sheltered her turned yellow and curled up into a dry tinder.

The poor little thing felt the cold bitterly, for her clothes were now in tatters and when snow came each flake was like a shovelful of snow to her. She tried to keep warm by wrapping herself in a dry leaf, but it was no good; she could not fight the cold.

Near the forest, a field which had been full of corn in the summer was now frozen and covered in stubble. The shivering maiden wandered into it, walked through the tree-like stubble and eventually came to the entrance of a fieldmouse's home.

The fieldmouse dwelt just under ground, in a cosy den, which contained a storeroom, a kitchen and a pretty dining-room. Thumbelina begged for a grain of barley, for she had not eaten for two days and she was very hungry.

The old fieldmouse had a kind heart. 'Poor little thing,' she said. 'Come and eat with me in the warm.'

She took an instant liking to Thumbelina and added, 'You are welcome to spend the winter here with me if you like, as long as you keep my den tidy for me and you tell me some stories. I am very fond of stories.'

The little maiden accepted the offer and found it most satisfactory.

One day the old mouse said: 'We are about to receive a visit from my neighbour; he comes regularly once a week. He is even better off than I am; he lives in a grand hall and wears a superb velvet coat. If you married him your fortune would be made. He is blind, so you must tell him your very best stories.

The idea of marrying the neighbour did not thrill Thumbelina, for he was a mole and could not talk about flowers or sunshine, for he had never seen them; all he had was wealth and learning. He came to pay his visit and Thumbelina sang him some songs. 'Ladybird, Ladybird, fly away home' among others; and the mole was delighted with her singing. The thought of marrying such a lovely singer appealed to him instantly but, being cautious by nature, he refrained from saying so at first.

He dug a long tunnel between his house and that of his neighbours and urged them to use it as often as they liked. He warned them not to be frightened by the dead bird which lay in the middle of the tunnel; the bird had obviously died recently and happened to have been buried just there.

When they went into the tunnel for the first time the mole came with them, with a piece of phosphorescent wood between his teeth to light the way. When they came to the dead bird he made a hole in the roof with his snout and daylight streamed into the tunnel; a swallow lay there with its wings tucked close to its body and it head and feet covered by feathers. It looked as if it had died of hunger. The sight greatly saddened Thumbelina, for she loved little birds; they had been such a comfort to her throughout the previous summer. The mole saw it differently. He shoved the swallow to one side and said, 'This one won't sing again! What a misfortune it is to be born a bird! Happily no child of mine will have such a sad fate. These creatures own nothing but a song; that is not sufficient to feed anyone in winter.'

'You are right, Mole,' the old mouse replied. 'Singing does not bring in much. It doesn't ward off cold and starvation, however soulful it may be.'

Thumbelina said nothing, but when the other two had gone on a little further, she bent down towards the bird, parted the feathers which covered its head and kissed it on its closed eyelids, saying, 'Maybe you are the one who sang so sweetly for me last summer, you poor little thing.'

The mole then closed up the hole and escorted the ladies back to their house. But that night Thumbelina couldn't sleep. She got up, wove a pretty rug out of odd bits of hay and went to cover the dead bird with it. She also put some thistledown she had found in the mouse's nest under its head, so that it could lie more comfortably on the cold earth.

'Farewell, beautiful bird, farewell,' she said, 'and thank you for your songs; they gave me much pleasure when all the trees were green and the sun shone brightly.' And she laid her head on its breast.

She quickly sprang up again, for a fluttering sound could be heard in the little heart. The swallow was not dead; it was just numbed with cold and the warmth of her hands had brought it back to life.

Swallows usually fly away in the autumn to warmer countries and those which delay are caught by the cold chill of winter. They fall unconscious to the ground and are soon covered by snow.

Thumbelina was rather alarmed for, compared to her, the bird seemed gigantic. But she quelled her fears. She put more thistledown around the bird, then went to fetch the mint leaf she used as a blanket and put it over the bird's head.

When she came back the following night it was still alive and it even opened its eyes briefly to look at the little maiden who stood there with some phosphorescent wood in her hand.

'Thank you, sweet child,' said the sick bird. 'You have done me good. Soon I shall be strong again and I will fly away on the rays of the sun.'

'Alas,' Thumbelina answered. 'It is cold outside; there is ice and snow and very little sun. You stay here and I will look after you.'

She brought some water in a flower petal and while he drank, the bird told her how he had torn one of his wings on a thorn bush and had been unable to follow his sister swallows to the South. He remembered falling to the ground and then nothing more.

All through that winter, without telling the mouse or the mole, Thumbelina looked after the bird and nursed it back to health. When spring came and the sunshine began to warm up the earth the swallow got ready to go. He urged Thumbelina to come with him; she could sit on his back, he said, and he would carry her all the way to the green forest. But Thumbelina knew that the old mouse would be very sad if she left her, so she declined the offer. She made a hole in the tunnel roof, as the mole had once done, and the swallow flew into the sunshine, saying: 'Adieu, Adieu, you good and loving child.' She watched him go with tears in her eyes, for she loved the swallow dearly. He gave one final tweet and was gone.

Thumbelina's sorrow was all the greater because she could not even see or feel the sunshine. The wheat grew as densely as a thick wood over the fieldmouse's den and it shut out the light.

The tedious mole had proposed and the old mouse decreed that Thumbelina should spend the summer preparing her trousseau. 'You must have a respectable quantity of clothes and linen if you are to marry Mr Mole,' she said.

The maiden was given a spindle to spin on and the mouse hired four hard-working spiders to do the weaving. Every night the mole would come and tell them all how much he disliked the summer which makes the earth so hot and hard and how much he longed for it to end, so that he could be married.

Every day, at daybreak and at sunset, Thumbelina went to the door of the den to look at the blue sky through the swaying wheat stalks, and every time she thought of her darling swallow who was so far away and might never come back.

By the time autumn came the trousseau was ready. 'In four weeks you will be married,' rejoiced the mouse. But the poor maiden cried, for she had no wish to marry the tedious mole.

'Don't be so foolish,' said the mouse. 'If you persist in your foolishness I shall have to bite some sense into you. You should be thrilled to marry such a handsome mole with such lavish storerooms and such an expensive fur coat.'

The day of the wedding arrived. The mole came to take Thumbelina to her underground home; once there she would never again see the sunshine, for he could not bear it. In the mouse's home the maiden could at least look at it from the doorway.

She went there for the last time, then lifted her hands up to the sky and in a forlorn voice she said, 'Farewell, lovely Sun, from my prison underground I shall never see you again.'

Then she took a few steps through the newly-cut stalks of wheat and kissed a little red flower. 'Farewell, little flower,' she said. 'If ever you should see my friend the swallow, give him my love.' At that moment she heard a joyous 'tweet' and, looking up, she saw the swallow flying overhead.

When he saw Thumbelina the bird was delighted. He tweeted repeatedly and flew towards his friend. She told him how she had been forced to consent to marry the ugly mole who lived underground, where the sun never shone and, as she spoke, her heart broke and she burst into tears.

The swallow tried to console her: 'Winter is coming and I am about to travel south to warmer lands. Why don't you come with me? You can climb on my back and fasten yourself on to me with your sash. Then we will fly away, far away from the ugly mole and his gloomy mansion, far beyond the mountains, to the place where the sun shines even more brightly than here, where it is forever summer and flowers bloom all the year round. Do come with me, dear Thumbelina, and let me repay you for saving my life when I was half-frozen to death.'

'Yes, I will go with you,' Thumbelina decided; and she settled herself on the swallow's back and tied her sash to his strongest feather. Then the swallow took off and they travelled over forests and seas and over high mountains covered in snow.

When she felt cold Thumbelina snuggled under the bird's warm feathers and just kept her head out so as to see the beautiful landscape, far down below.

At last they reached the warm lands where green and purple grapes grow wild along the hedges, where lemon and orange groves abound and where the scent of a thousand flowers fills the air. Children skipped along the country lanes and played with butterflies of many colours.

The swallow stopped on the shore of a blue lake, near a marble palace of great antiquity which was adorned with a colonnade. A vine grew between the columns and many birds had built their nests there.

100

This was where the swallow lived. 'Welcome to my home,' he said
to Thumbelina, 'but I fear you would not be comfortable enough
in this nest. We must find you a more suitable dwelling. Choose a
flower which appeals to you and I will settle you there. I do so want
you to have an agreeable stay here.'

'This is all wonderful,' exclaimed Thumbelina, clapping her
hands with joy.

The swallow set her down on a broad leaf among some beautiful
white flowers which grew in the cracks of a broken column which
lay on the ground.

Thumbelina was feasting her eyes on all the beauties around her
when, to her intense surprise, she saw a tiny man, as pale and trans-
lucent as glass, standing inside the flower beside her. On his head
he wore a golden crown and on his shoulders a pair of tiny wings.

He was the spirit of the flower and he ruled over all the other
flower-spirits around.

'What a handsome prince,' whispered Thumbelina to the swallow.

At the sight of the gigantic bird, the little prince was slightly alarmed but he soon recovered when he saw Thumbelina. He thought she was the most beautiful maiden in the whole world and instantly fell in love with her. He placed his crown on her head, enquired about her name and asked if she would consent to become his wife.

There was a big difference between this proposal of marriage and those of the ugly toad and the boring mole. To this one she consented gladly and so became the queen of flowers.

Tiny maidens and tiny sprites came out from every flower to bring her wedding gifts.

The one she liked most of all was a pair of diaphanous wings which had formerly belonged to a large white fly. They fitted perfectly on her shoulders and thanks to them she was able to fly from flower to flower.

As for the king, he decreed that she would no longer be called Thumbelina. 'It is an ugly name,' he said, 'and it does not suit somebody as beautiful as you. The queen of flowers should have a regal name. From now on you will be called Queen Maia.'

Meanwhile, the swallow in his nest sang his sweetest song; but deep in his heart he felt sad at the thought that soon he would have to depart and leave his little friend.

'Adieu, Adieu,' he sang when he flew north again, back to Denmark. And all through that summer he sang of his adventures and of Thumbelina.

His nest was directly above the window of a writer of fairy tales and that is how this writer learnt the story of the tiny little maiden.

THE EMPEROR'S NEW CLOTHES

A long time ago there lived an emperor who was so fond of clothes that he spent all his fortune on them. His only concern, when he inspected his troops, attended plays or just went for a stroll, was to show off his latest outfit. At every hour of the day he would change into a new suit of clothes and people would say 'the Emperor is in his dressing-room', in the way one would normally have said 'he is in the Council Chamber'. The imperial city was full of bustle and noise because of the many foreign merchants who came there to trade and one day two swindlers came into the city disguised as weavers. They declared that they could weave the most magnificent cloth in the world. Besides its remarkable pattern and colour, this cloth had an absolutely unique quality: any clothes made out of it were invisible to people who were bad at their job or just plain stupid.

'Such clothes would be exceedingly useful,' thought the emperor. 'They would enable me to find out whether I have any incompetent ministers and to sort out the clever ones from the stupid ones. I must definitely have some of this cloth.'

He gave the two swindlers a generous sum of money and ordered them to start weaving immediately.

The crooks set up two looms and pretended to work at them, when in fact there was nothing at all on the shuttles. They asked for more fine silk and fine gold thread and pretended to work at the looms late into the night, even though there was nothing on them.

The emperor was dying to know how they were getting on.

But he was a little worried by the thought that incompetent or stupid people were unable to see the cloth. He obviously did not think such a thing could happen to him, but just to be on the safe side he decided to send someone else to examine the cloth before he did. Everyone in the city had heard of the cloth's marvellous property and all were keen to see its effects.

In the end the king decided to send his most trusted minister, for he knew the man to be both wise and competent and, therefore, such a man could not fail to be a good judge.

The old man entered the room where the looms were set up and opened his eyes very wide. 'Dear me,' he thought, 'I cannot see anything.' However, he was too wise to say so aloud.

The two swindlers urged him to come nearer, to have a better look at the pattern and to see the colour in a better light. The old man looked where they told him to look, but he could see nothing, for the simple reason that there was nothing to see.

'Oh dear,' he thought, 'could it be that I am stupid and incompetent? If so, nobody must suspect it. I must never admit that I cannot see this cloth.'

'Well, what do you think of it?' asked one of the weavers.

'I think it is quite charming,' the old man replied, peering through his glasses at the invisible cloth. 'What a lovely pattern and what sumptuous colours. I shall tell the emperor that I am well-pleased with it.'

'We are delighted to hear it,' said the weavers and they proceeded to describe the imaginary pattern in great detail. The old minister listened carefully, so as to be able to repeat it all accurately to the emperor.

The villains went on asking for money, for silk and for gold thread, saying that large quantities were required for their product; but of course they just pocketed the lot and kept the looms empty.

A few days later the emperor sent another dignitary to inspect the cloth and see if it was nearly ready. But he, like the old minister, could see nothing.

'Isn't this cloth fantastic?' the weavers said as they pointed out to him the intricacies of the invisible pattern and the beauty of its colours.

'This is extraordinary,' thought the dignitary. 'I know very well that I am not stupid; therefore this must mean that I am not good at my job. However that may be, I shall do all I can to keep it.'

So he warmly praised the cloth and showed great admiration for its pattern and colour.

'It is the most magnificent cloth I have ever seen,' he said to the emperor; and from then on the whole city spoke of nothing else.

After this the emperor decided to go and look at the cloth while it was still on the loom. Followed by his many courtiers, including the minister and the dignitary, he went to visit the crafty weavers at their work.

'Isn't it magnificent?' said the minister and the dignitary. 'Both the pattern and the colours are worthy of Your Majesty.'

And they pointed to the loom as if there had been something on it.

'What is the matter with me?' thought the emperor. 'I cannot see anything. Could it be that I am a simpleton and that I am not fit to govern? O, woe is me! This is the worst misfortune possible.' And aloud he said, 'Magnificent, magnificent! I could not be more delighted.'

He nodded repeatedly to show his satisfaction and gazed at the empty loom with a delighted look on his face. Naturally, his courtiers followed suit and all expressed much admiration for the cloth they could not see. They even suggested that the emperor should have a suit made out of it for the great procession which was due to take place shortly thereafter. 'Fantastic! Beautiful! Magnificent!' and many similar adjectives were used to describe the wondrous cloth.

As for the two impostors, they were given a medal and the title of 'gentleman-weavers.'

The night before the procession they showed renewed zeal by staying up all night and burning sixteen candles. They pretended to take the cloth off the loom, then went through the motions of cutting and sewing, by snapping their scissors into thin air and threading their needles with invisible thread. Finally they announced that the new clothes were ready.

The emperor set forth immediately, with his equerries, to examine them.

The villains held their arms up as if they were holding something precious and explained to the emperor what they were holding.

'Here we have the coat; here is the cape and now the trousers. As you can see, these garments are light as a feather and you will find them wonderfully comfortable. They feel exactly as if one had nothing on.'

'Indeed,' said the equerries, who could see nothing, since there was nothing to see.

'If Your Imperial Highness should care to take his clothes off,' the rogues went on, 'and try his new ones on in front of the mirror?'

The emperor took all his clothes off and put on the new ones, one by one – or so he thought. Then they pretended to attach the ceremonial train round his waist and the emperor turned from side to side to admire the effect in the mirror.

'What a wonderful fit! What a beautiful cut! What gorgeous colours!' the courtiers exclaimed.

Then the master of ceremonies came in to announce that the imperial canopy was outside and that the procession could start.

'Very well,' said the emperor. 'I am quite ready and I feel truly fine in this new outfit.'

He twirled once more in front of the mirror, to show how much he liked the outfit. Then his chamberlains picked up the invisible train, held it up in the air and the procession started.

As the emperor proceeded through the city in great pomp, all his subjects, in the streets and at the windows, cried out, 'What a wonderful outfit! What a gorgeous train! What a perfect fit!' for nobody wanted to admit that they could not see anything. So as not to be thought stupid or bad at their job they all praised the new clothes as loudly as they could.

In the middle of this concert of adulation a small child suddenly spoke out:

'But he has nothing on!'

'Listen to the voice of innocence,' the father said.

What the child had said was whispered through the crowd until everybody knew about it; and all the people said in unison, 'He has nothing on!'

The emperor was highly mortified, all the more so since he knew perfectly well that it was true. But, with great dignity, he decided that, true or not, the procession must go on and he went on walking with his head held high, while his chamberlains held up in the air his non-existent train.